Karen's Gift

**Other books by
Ann M. Martin**

P. S. Longer Letter Later
(written with Paula Danziger)
Leo the Magnificat
Rachel Parker, Kindergarten Show-off
Eleven Kids, One Summer
Ma and Pa Dracula
Yours Turly, Shirley
Ten Kids, No Pets
With You and Without You
Me and Katie (the Pest)
Stage Fright
Inside Out
Bummer Summer

For older readers:

Missing Since Monday
Just a Summer Romance
Slam Book

THE BABY-SITTERS CLUB series
THE BABY-SITTERS CLUB mysteries
THE KIDS IN MS. COLMAN'S CLASS series
BABY-SITTERS LITTLE SISTER series
(see inside book covers for a complete listing)

Little Sister

Karen's Gift
Ann M. Martin

Illustrations by Susan Crocca Tang

A
LITTLE APPLE
PAPERBACK

SCHOLASTIC INC.
New York Toronto London Auckland Sydney
Mexico City New Delhi Hong Kong

ISBN 0-590-52527-1

Copyright © 2000 by Ann M. Martin. Illustrations copyright © 2000 by Scholastic Inc. All rights reserved. Published by Scholastic Inc. THE BABY-SITTERS LITTLE SISTER, LITTLE APPLE PAPERBACKS, and associated logos are trademarks and/or registered trademarks of Scholastic Inc.

12 11 10 9 8 7 6 5 4 3 2 1   0 1 2 3 4 5/0

Printed in the U.S.A.   40
First Scholastic printing, July 2000

The author gratefully acknowledges
Stephanie Calmenson
for her help
with this book.

Karen's Gift

1

An Exciting Job

*D*ingdong! *Woof! Woof! Dingdong! Woof!*

It was a Monday afternoon, the first day of May. I was ringing the doorbell at my neighbors' house. I had to ring twice because I did not think anyone could hear it the first time. There was too much barking inside. Finally the door opened.

Duke, the Hsus' golden retriever, trotted up to greet me. He is a gentle old dog with gray around his muzzle.

"Hello, Karen!" said Mrs. Hsu. "Duke and I are both happy to see you."

The Hsu family are my big-house neighbors. (I have two houses. A big house and a little house. I will tell you more about them later.) The people in the Hsu family are Scott, who is seven like me, Timmy, who is five, and Mr. and Mrs. Hsu. Mrs. Hsu was the only one home that afternoon.

"I am so glad you will be able to walk Duke while we are out of town," she said. "Come inside. I will give you the key and show you where things are."

I followed Mrs. Hsu into the house. This was going to be an exciting job. I love exciting jobs!

Wait a minute. I have told you about the Hsus. But I have not told you about me yet. My name is Karen Brewer. I have blonde hair, blue eyes, and freckles. Also, I am a glasses-wearer. I wear blue glasses for reading. I wear pink glasses the rest of the time.

Slurp! Slurp! Duke stopped following me around long enough to get a drink of water.

"Here are our keys, Karen. On the way

out I will show you how to use them," said Mrs. Hsu.

She showed me where Duke's leash is kept. It was red with black paw prints on it. Then she showed me where to find Duke's treats.

"I usually give him one after his walk," said Mrs. Hsu. "Speaking of treats, we keep the people treats in this cabinet, in case you are hungry when you come over."

"Thank you," I replied. "Duke and I can have snack time together."

Mrs. Hsu smiled.

"How about taking a walk around the block with Duke and me? That way you can see where he likes to go," said Mrs. Hsu.

We went from tree to bush to lamppost. Duke carefully sniffed every one. When he stopped to do his business, Mrs. Hsu cleaned up after him with a plastic bag.

"I will give you a supply of these," she said. "That way we can keep the neighborhood nice and clean."

3

When we got back to the Hsus' house, I took Duke's leash off and we washed up. Then Mrs. Hsu gave me a homemade oatmeal-raisin cookie and showed me how to use the keys.

"I will be here every day you're gone, right after school!" I said.

I petted Duke, waved good-bye, and walked off with the keys in my pocket. I felt gigundoly grown-up. I, Karen Brewer, had an important job. And I was going to be paid very well to do it.

As I walked home, I thought about the things I could buy with the money I would earn. I could buy myself a car, I thought. Or maybe I could buy a house!

I was just having fun. I did not really think my dog-walking money would buy those things. And I already had enough houses. Oh, I promised to tell you about the two houses I live in. I will do that now.

2

Two Houses

Here is the story of how I came to have two houses. And two mommies. And two daddies. And even two dogs.

A long time ago when I was little, the people in my family were Mommy, Daddy, my little brother Andrew (he is four going on five), and me. We all lived together in a big house in Stoneybrook, Connecticut.

But Mommy and Daddy began having a lot of trouble getting along. It was a sad time. They tried their best to work things out, but they could not do it. They explained to Andrew and me that they loved each of us very much and always would. But they did not want to be married to each other. Then they got divorced.

Mommy moved out with Andrew and me to a little house not far away. She met a very nice man named Seth. Mommy and Seth got married and now Seth is my stepfather.

So the people in my little-house family are Mommy, Seth, Andrew, and me. Our pets are Emily Junior, my pet rat; Bob, Andrew's hermit crab; Midgie, Seth's dog, who is now our family dog; and Rocky, Seth's cat, who is now our family cat.

Daddy stayed in the big house after he and Mommy got divorced. (It is the house he grew up in.) He met and married a very nice woman named Elizabeth. Now Elizabeth is my stepmother.

Elizabeth was married once before she married Daddy, and has four children. They are my stepbrothers and stepsister. David Michael is seven like me. Kristy is thirteen and the best stepsister ever. (She is also president of a club she started with her friends. It is called the Baby-sitters Club.) Sam and Charlie are so old they are in high school.

I also have a little sister, Emily Michelle, who is two and a half. I love her a lot, which is why I named my rat after her. Daddy and Elizabeth adopted Emily from a far-away country called Vietnam.

The other person living at the big house is Nannie. She is Elizabeth's mother, which makes her my stepgrandmother. She came to live at the big house to help with Emily. But she helps with everyone.

Now, here are the pets at the big house: Shannon, David Michael's big Bernese mountain dog puppy; Pumpkin, our new black kitten; Crystal Light the Second, my goldfish; and Goldfishie, Andrew's you-know-what.

Andrew and I switch houses almost every month. We usually spend one month at the big house, then one month at the little house. (This month was a big-house month.)

To make the switching easier, we have two of lots of things. Andrew and I have two of so many things that I gave us special names. I call us Andrew Two-Two and Karen Two-Two. (I thought up those names after my teacher read a book to our class. It was called *Jacob Two-Two Meets the Hooded Fang*.) We have two bicycles, one at each house. We have two sets of toys and clothes and books. And of course, we have our two families.

I also have two best friends. Hannie Papadakis lives across the street and one house over from the big house. Nancy Dawes lives next door to the little house. (We are all in the same second-grade class at Stoneybrook Academy.)

By the way, having two houses means having two sets of keys. And if you add in the keys I got today, I have three sets of keys! I better not carry them all at the same time. I would jingle and jangle so much that everyone in town would have to cover their ears!

3

Hands Up!

On Tuesday, while we were waiting in our classroom for our teacher, I told Hannie and Nancy about my dog-walking job.

"If my family ever goes away, we could hire you to walk Noodle for us," said Hannie. (Noodle is Hannie's poodle.)

"Have you decided what you are going to do with the money you make?" asked Nancy.

"Not yet. But I will think of something," I replied.

Just then Ms. Colman arrived.

"Good morning, class," she said. "Please be seated."

I am so lucky Ms. Colman is my teacher! She is the nicest, most interesting teacher a second-grader could have. She never raises her voice, even when I do things some other teachers might get upset about. For example, a lot of times I forget to raise my hand and I call out pretty loudly. Ms. Colman just reminds me to use my indoor voice.

That is not all. Sometimes she gives me important jobs to do. (You *know* I love important jobs!) Today she asked me to take attendance.

I checked my own name off first. Then I checked off Nancy and Hannie, who waved to me from the back of the room. (I used to sit in the back with them. But Ms. Colman moved me up front when I got my glasses so I could see better.)

I checked off Hank Reubens, who also sits in the back.

I checked off my best enemy, Pamela Harding. She can be a meanie-mo sometimes. Her friends are Jannie Gilbert and Leslie Morris. They were in class too.

So was Addie Sidney. She sits in the front of the room. She has a wheelchair with its own desk.

Natalie Springer sits on one side of me. I did not see her. But I knew she was in class. (She was bending down to pick up her drooping socks.) I checked off her name.

Ricky Torres sits on the other side of me. (He is my pretend husband. We got married on the playground one day at recess.) I checked off his name.

I checked off Bobby Gianelli, Omar Harris, and Audrey Green. I checked off Terri and Tammy Barkan, who are twins.

I checked off a few more names. Check, check. Then I handed the book and pencil back to Ms. Colman.

Knock, knock. I looked at the door. Mr. Mackey was there.

"Yippee!" I called out.

"Indoor voice, please, Karen," said Ms. Colman.

12

Mr. Mackey is our art teacher. He goes from room to room with his art cart. We settled down and waited to hear what we were going to be working on.

"I have a new project in mind for today," said Mr. Mackey. "Everyone, please raise your hand."

We did not know why he wanted us to raise our hands. But we followed his instructions.

"Your hands are your art projects," said Mr. Mackey.

Hmm. This sounded interesting.

"During my next few visits you will be making a papier-mâché model of one of your hands," he said. "When it is dry, you will paint pictures on it. The pictures will tell us who you are."

"Do you mean we have to paint pictures of ourselves?" asked Tammy.

"You can if you like. But you can also draw pictures of things that you are interested in," Mr. Mackey replied. "If you like to play baseball, you could draw a bat and a

ball. If you have a pet you love, you could draw the face of your pet. Take some time to think about what you would like to draw. When you are ready, you can start making some sketches."

I looked at my hand and tried to think what I would like to draw on it. But as hard as I tried, all I could see was my plain old hand.

"I am going to draw a picture of myself to give my mother for Mother's Day," said Natalie.

"I am sure she will like that," I replied.

It was not something I wanted to do. But thinking about Mother's Day helped me answer Nancy's question. I knew what I would buy with my dog-walking money. I would buy a really great gift for Mommy.

"Thanks, Natalie!" I said.

"I do not know what I did," she replied. "But you are welcome."

4

Karen's Plan

School was fun. But I could hardly wait to get home. It was the first day of my dog-walking job.

I used the keys just the way Mrs. Hsu had showed me. Through the window, I could see Duke. His tail was wagging wildly. He was excited to hear the key in the door.

When I walked inside, he raced to me and leaned against my legs. I scratched him behind his ears. Then he lay down and rolled over.

"Come on, we are going for your walk," I said.

He popped back up.

"Woof!"

I clipped his paw-print leash to his collar, and we went for our walk around the block. Nice and slow. Lots of sniffing. Cleaning up with baggies. (Guess what. That was my least favorite part of the job.)

Then I walked Duke to Hannie's house. Mrs. Hsu said the more exercise Duke got, the better. And Hannie said Duke and Noodle got along very well.

Hannie and I took turns throwing a ball for Noodle and Duke to fetch. They played the game like this: Duke fetched the ball. Noodle ran after Duke and barked a lot.

I had already told Hannie my idea about using the money I earned to buy a gift for Mommy. Now I was trying to think of what that gift should be.

"I just thought of something," said Hannie. "You will need to buy a gift for Elizabeth too."

"You are right," I replied. "But how am I going to make enough money at one job to buy two presents?"

"I do not know," said Hannie. "Anything nice is sure to be expensive. Maybe you should make gifts instead."

"No. This year I want to do something different. I want to buy gifts with money that I earn myself. But presents are expensive, and now I have two presents to buy. There is only one thing to do. I will just have to walk two dogs."

"But what other dog are you going to walk? Most families do not go away in May," said Hannie.

Hmm. Hannie was right. I needed a plan. It was getting late anyway. So I decided to go home and have a talk with Daddy.

"See you later," I said.

I walked Duke home and gave him a treat. (I did not take a cookie for myself because I had already eaten a snack at Hannie's house.) I carefully locked the door. When I peered through the window, Duke was looking back at me. He looked sad. I was glad the house sitter would be home in just a few hours. (The Hsus had hired someone to feed Duke and to sleep over so Duke would not be alone all night.)

When I got home, Daddy was in the den reading. Daddy works at home most days. His office is downstairs.

"Hi, Karen," he said. "How was your first dog-walking day?"

"It was fun," I replied. "I took Duke to Hannie's house. He and Noodle played together. But there is something I need to talk to you about."

I told him my problem.

"I need another dog-walking job. But it might be hard to find one. People do not go away much in May."

"Someone who works might still need your help with a dog," said Daddy. "People worry about leaving their dogs alone all day."

"You are right!" I said. "I will ask around in the neighborhood."

"I am glad you are enjoying your job. Just remember to leave enough time for your homework," said Daddy. "And of course you'll want to leave time to see your friends."

"I will leave time," I said.

I was glad I had talked to Daddy. Now I had a very good plan.

A Friend in Need

On Wednesday morning Ms. Colman chose Hank to take attendance. Hank is pretty nice. He is smart too.

"Thank you, Hank," said Ms. Colman when he had finished. "Class, I have been looking at the calendar for the weeks ahead, and I see we have a holiday coming up."

"Mother's Day!" I called out. Oops.

"Raise your hand, please, Karen," said Ms. Colman. "But you are right. Mother's Day is coming up. Is there anything you would like to do in class for this holiday?"

Natalie raised her hand.

"I am going to give the papier-mâché hand to my mother as a present," she said.

"That is a good idea," said Ms. Colman. She called on Addie next.

"Can we make Mother's Day cards in class?" asked Addie.

"Sure," said Ms. Colman. "Anything else?"

Ms. Colman called on Pamela.

"Can we have a Mother's Day party?" asked Pamela.

Ooh! I hate to admit it. But my best enemy had a very good idea. Ms. Colman thought so too.

"I like that idea very much," she said. "All in favor of the party, raise your hands."

I looked around the room. Almost every hand was up. Natalie's hand was not up because she was under the desk again pulling up her socks. And I did not see Hank's hand raised. But just about everyone else seemed excited about the idea.

"I know that many mothers work and

will not be able to come. So feel free to invite other people — aunts, cousins, special friends," said Ms. Colman. "We can make up invitations this afternoon and have the party a week from Friday."

We talked a little more about the party and decided we would make a display of work we are proud of. Then we broke into our book-talk groups. I am in a group with Hank, Sara, and Omar. Every month each group reads a different book. At the end of the month we give reports to the class. My group is reading a book of Greek myths. They are very exciting.

Hank and I were waiting for Sara and Omar. (They were having trouble finding their books.)

"I am glad we are having a party," I said. "It will be fun."

"It would be fun if I had someone to bring," said Hank.

He seemed sad. Then I remembered something. Hank's parents are divorced, like mine. Only he is not lucky enough to

have two houses in the same town. Hank's mother moved all the way to Florida to be with the rest of her family. He and his sisters stayed in Stoneybrook with their father.

"Ms. Colman said we do not have to invite our mothers," I reminded him. "I am sure we do not have to have any guest at all."

"I would like a guest," said Hank. "But I cannot think of anyone who can come."

Hmm. I have a very big family. I was sure I could think of someone for Hank to invite. Mommy would be my guest. (She works, but only part-time.) Elizabeth probably could not come because she works full-time. Nannie! That was it!

"I am sure you could borrow my step-grandmother, Nannie. She is really nice. I could ask her for you," I said.

Just then, Omar and Sara showed up with their books. Hank smiled and gave me the thumbs-up sign.

"Thanks, Karen," he said.

6

Dogs and More Dogs!

After school, I did not have time to think about mothers or Mother's Day. I had dogs on my mind.

First I went to the Hsus' house. Duke was very happy to see me again. His tail wagged so fast, I thought it was going to fly off of him!

I took him for his walk around the block. But something happened that had not happened before. A squirrel crossed Duke's path.

"Woof!"

Duke chased the squirrel to a tree. I held on tight to the leash and ran with him.

We watched the squirrel race high up in the tree. When Duke saw that it was not coming down, he started sniffing the ground again. I hoped we would not see any more squirrels soon.

We finished our walk around the block. But I did not take Duke home. I decided that he was a good advertisement. Since he looked very happy, I was sure he would help me get another dog-walking job in the neighborhood.

"Come on, Duke. You are going to help me get another job," I said.

I walked him to the Kilbournes' house. (Their dog, Astrid, is the mother of David Michael's puppy, Shannon.)

Dingdong! Woof! Woof! Woof!

Mrs. Kilbourne came to the door.

"Hi!" I said. "As you can see from this happy dog, I have started a dog-walking business. Do you need me to walk Astrid for you after school?"

Mrs. Kilbourne laughed.

"As a matter of fact, we were just talking about getting a dog walker," said Mrs. Kilbourne.

"You were?" I asked. I could not believe it!

"We are all so busy during the week. We do not have enough time to walk Astrid for as long as she needs," said Mrs. Kilbourne.

"I can start on Friday," I said. (Kristy had promised to take me shopping on Thursday.)

"That would be fine," said Mrs. Kilbourne.

I told her my dog-walking rate. She said that was fine too. Yippcc!

That was so easy I decided to see if I could find another dog to walk.

I went to Melody Korman's house. Her family has a brand-new beagle puppy named Maggie. Mr. Korman said he would love to hire me as a dog-walker. That is because puppies have a lot of energy and need lots of walks.

I was doing so well that I could not stop. Maybe I would get lucky again. I decided to try one more house. We had some new neighbors. I had met them twice, but I did not know if they had any pets. I knocked on their door. I heard barking. Yes!! They had two little terriers named Gracie and Garbo. For a two-dog walk, they were going to pay me one and a half times my regular rate.

I decided I was an excellent business-woman. I had just started my business and already I had five dogs to walk. That seemed like plenty. If I needed more, I could sign them up later.

I was sure I would be able to make enough money to buy excellent gifts for Mommy and Elizabeth by Mother's Day.

7

Window-shopping

On Thursday, Kristy kept her promise and took me shopping downtown after I finished my dog-walking job.

"Can you believe how many dogs I am going to be walking?" I said. "Maybe someday I will have a business with my friends. It will be just like your Baby-sitters Club. But my club will be the Dog-Walkers Club!"

"You will have to be very organized and responsible," said Kristy.

"I know. I have been very responsible so far," I replied.

"Really? How many days have you been walking dogs?" asked Kristy.

"Two!" I said.

Kristy laughed. "I guess that is a good start. Do you have a work planner yet? And where do you keep your doggie bags?"

"I do not have a planner. And I have been stuffing the doggie bags into my pocket," I replied.

"Come on. We can check out the stationery department at Bellair's department store," said Kristy. "They should have what you need."

Kristy was right. We found the perfect pocket planner and a pouch that was just right for holding doggie bags. I also bought a small box of colored pencils. That was my idea. I could use a different color pencil to write each dog's name in my planning book.

"Now you are thinking like an organized businesswoman," said Kristy.

I had to use my savings to buy everything. But I was not worried. I knew I would make the money back by the next week. Maybe I would have some left over to buy presents for other people. Maybe I could even buy a present for me.

We went downstairs to do some browsing. I saw a beautiful sparkly bracelet that would look excellent on Elizabeth. I saw a scarf that I was sure Mommy would love.

I noticed that Kristy liked some socks. Maybe I would buy them for her. (And for me too.) And there was a hat that would look nice on Nannie. (And on me too!)

I imagined buying up the whole store.

"We better head back," said Kristy. "It is getting late."

When I got home, I filled in my planner using my neatest handwriting. Then I stuffed doggie bags into my pouch. I was ready for Friday's dog-walking duty.

At dinner my family made a plan for Mother's Day. We decided to fix a brunch for Elizabeth and Nannie. Andrew and I would visit Mommy later in the day.

"Remember, neither one of you is allowed to do any work next Sunday," Daddy said to Nannie and Elizabeth. "It will be your day to sit back and relax."

"I will like that just fine," said Nannie.

"Me too," said Elizabeth. "I cannot wait."

8

Poor Hank

"Please pass the paste, Natalie," I said.

It was Friday. Mr. Mackey was helping us with our papier-mâché hands. I was about to dip my first strip of newspaper into a paste made of flour and water when Hank sat down beside me. Uh-oh.

"Did you ask?" he whispered.

I knew just what he was talking about, and I felt bad. I had completely forgotten to talk to Nannie about coming to the party.

"I am sorry. I have not asked Nannie yet," I replied.

35

I was starting to wonder if this was such a good idea after all. Remembering to ask Nannie was one more job for me to do. And I was very busy these days. So was Nannie.

I thought about telling Hank that he would have to ask someone else to the party. But when I looked at his face, I could not do it. I could tell this was really important to him. Poor Hank.

Natalie stood up to get more newspaper.

"I will ask Nannie. I promise," I said.

I took out my new pocket planner. I made a note to talk to Nannie.

"Thank you," said Hank.

"You are welcome," I replied.

Hank looked relieved. That made me feel good. I decided to do even better.

"If Nannie cannot come, I promise to find you someone else!" I said.

Hank smiled and gave me another thumbs-up sign as Natalie returned. Then he dipped a paper strip into the bowl of paste. I smiled back and dipped a paper strip too. Natalie was faster than either of us. The top of her hand was already half covered.

"This is so gooey!" she said.

I put my first gooey strip across the top of my left hand.

"I like it. It feels cool," I said.

Hank put a strip on his hand. Then another. And another. Then he curled his fingers and reached out to me.

"I am a papier-mâché mummy!" he said.

"We should make papier-mâché models of our whole bodies. Then we could have a happy Mummy's Day party!" I said.

Natalie, Hank, and I had a good time working on our art projects together. When the backs of our hands were covered with layers and layers of gooey strips, we walked around visiting other tables. Everyone in our class was waiting for their molds to dry partway. As soon as they were dry enough, we could take the molds off.

Finally they were ready. We lined them up on the windowsills.

"You all did very well today," said Mr.

Mackey. "Remember to put a name tag next to your model."

We made name tags. Then we cleaned ourselves and our classroom.

"I will see you next week. Then you can start drawing on your hands," said Mr. Mackey.

9

Woof!

After school on Friday I dropped off my school bag.

It was my first five-dog working day.

"Would you like a snack?" asked Nannie.

"No, thank you," I replied. "I will have a snack with Duke."

Duke was the first dog on my list. We went for our usual walk around the block.

"Um, could you please walk faster and sniff less today?" I said to him. "I have a few other dogs to walk."

Duke is a smart dog. But he did not seem

to understand me. He walked and sniffed as slowly as ever. (I was glad there were no squirrels.)

When we returned to the Hsus' house, I gave Duke his treat and gulped down a glass of milk with a cookie.

"See you tomorrow," I said. "Wait! I almost forgot."

I picked up an envelope waiting on the hall table with my name on it. Mrs. Hsu had said to take it on Friday. Today was my first payday. I put the envelope into my pouch.

"Thank you, Duke," I said.

I headed for the Kilbournes' house. Mrs. Kilbourne put on Astrid's leash and handed it to me. Astrid was not the fastest walker in the world either. But she did not stop to sniff as much as Duke had.

While we walked, I thought about the envelope in my pouch and what I would buy with it. There was always that bracelet for Elizabeth and scarf for Mommy. But maybe I would find something even more exciting.

Astrid did her business. I cleaned up and

dropped her back at the Kilbournes' house.

The Kormans' house was next. No one answered when I rang the bell. I followed my instructions and got the key from under the back-door mat.

Maggie, the beagle puppy, was in her crate.

"Come, Maggie," I said. "It is time for your walk."

She was so excited that she made a puddle right there and then.

"I wish you had waited," I said. "But you will learn."

On her walk, Maggie went after everything that moved. She jumped after butterflies and raced after bugs.

I was glad the Kormans were home when I returned. I did not like to leave Maggie all alone.

My next stop was at Gracie and Garbo's house.

"Woof! Woof! Woof! Woof!"

They began barking as soon as I started up the walk to their house.

Their owners, Mr. and Mrs. Henry, opened the door. The dogs' leashes were already clipped to their collars.

"They are excited about their walk," said Mr. Henry.

"If Gracie gets stubborn, just give her a little push," said Mrs. Henry.

We were halfway around the block when Gracie got stubborn. I pushed. It did not work. I pulled the leash a little. It did not work. Then a boy skated by us.

"Woof, woof, woof, woof, woof!"

Gracie and Garbo both tried to take off after him. I was glad they were small dogs. They were much easier to hold on to than Duke was.

Gracie forgot about being stubborn and we finished our walk.

After I dropped Gracie and Garbo at their house, I checked my planner to make sure I was not forgetting any dogs. I had walked them all. But there was one thing I still needed to do. I needed to ask Nannie about the party.

When I got home, I ran into David Michael.

"You are a mess!" he said.

I knew he was right. Baggies were popping out of my pouch. My T-shirt was hanging out of my jeans. My hands were covered with dirt. I was sure my face was too. But I did not care. I had had fun walking the dogs.

"You are just jealous because I am making money," I said to David Michael.

Then I went to the kitchen, where Nannie was getting dinner ready. I told her about the party and Hank and asked if she could come.

"I wish I could join you. But I already have plans for that day," said Nannie. "Please tell Hank I am sorry."

I was disappointed, but not too worried. There was still time to find another guest for Hank. I would just have to think a little harder.

10

Grrr!

"Do not forget!" said Hannie. "Be at my house at four-thirty."

"I will try my best," I replied.

It was Monday. The kids in my class were excited about the after-school special that would be on television that afternoon. It was the first of a three-part mystery series. I am very good at solving mysteries. I wanted to be there to watch it with my friends. But I had dogs to walk first.

I needed a plan to make my job go faster. In no time I thought of a very good one. The dogs I was walking are all friendly. I was sure they would get along with one another. So I decided to walk more than one dog at a time.

I picked up Astrid first. She is big, like Duke. I would walk them together. We headed for Duke's house.

Woof! Woof! He barked when he heard us coming.

"I brought you a friend, Duke!" I said.

When we got inside, Astrid went straight for Duke's food bowl.

Grrr. Duke did not like that. I picked up the food bowl. Then I tried to put on Duke's leash. But I could not catch him. He and Astrid were racing around the house. Duke may be old but he can move fast when he wants to.

Crash! Oops. A candy dish was knocked off the coffee table. Luckily it did not break.

"Duke, come!" I called. No Duke. I tried calling again. This time I made sure I had two treats in my hand.

"Duke, come!"

Duke smelled the treats and came running. Astrid was right behind him. I quickly put on Duke's leash. Then I gave each dog a treat and took them outside.

I looked at my watch. Boo. I was trying to save time by walking two dogs at once. But it had taken much longer to get them out of the house than I had thought it would.

"We need to walk fast," I told the dogs. "I have an after-school special to watch."

Duke and Astrid were not walking fast. They were not walking at all. They were rolling around on the ground playing. And getting dirty. And making me late!

I gave a quick pull on their leashes, but they did not even notice. If I had brought treats, they might have listened to me. But I did not have any. I called and called. They acted like they did not even hear me.

I had to wait until they were tired of playing. Then I walked them around the block.

Sniff. Sniff. They both sniffed a lot. Then it was time to pick up after Duke. Then I picked up after Astrid. More playing. More sniffing. More playing. More sniffing.

"Please come home. Please?" I said. "It is almost four o'clock, and I still have three dogs to walk."

It took a long time. But finally I had taken each of them home.

My next dog team was Maggie, Gracie, and Garbo. I hoped I could get them to move a little faster than Astrid and Duke. I could not.

I picked up Gracie and Garbo first. We were halfway down the street when Gracie started her imitation of a tree. She would not move.

"Please," I said. "Please? Please!"

I wished again that I had dog biscuits with me. Maybe that would have made her move. But I did not have any. I decided the only way to get her to move was to move her myself. I was glad she was not very big.

I picked her up and did not put her down till we reached Maggie's house.

Maggie was so excited to have company that she made puddles all the way down the Kormans' sidewalk. Then she jumped on Garbo's head.

Grrr. Garbo did not like that. And when Garbo growled, Maggie dropped down and rolled over onto her back.

"Maggie, get up," I said.

She stayed where she was until Gracie yipped at her.

Maggie was up. But she would not walk. None of the dogs would. They wanted to play, just like Astrid and Duke.

I looked at my watch. Four-thirty. Hannie and Nancy were sitting in front of the TV. And I still had three dogs to walk and take back home. I was going to miss the TV special and an afternoon with my friends. *Grrr.*

It was no use hurrying the dogs. I decided that they might as well have a good time, even though I could not. At least I would be making money for my trouble. I would be making enough money to buy two excellent gifts for Mommy and Elizabeth. Maybe I would buy them each a beautiful china dog. They would be pretty to look at. And china dogs do not have to be walked!

Disappointing News

After dinner, Mommy called. She asked how I was. I told her about my day of dog-walking. (I had told her that I had a new job. But I had not told her I was going to use the money I earned to buy her a present.) I also told her about missing the show.

"I am sorry you did not get to watch the after-school special with your friends," said Mommy. "But I am sure it will be repeated. If I see it listed, I will let you know."

"Thank you," I replied.

"Karen, I have a good-news reason and a

bad-news reason for calling," said Mommy. "The good news is that a famous jewelry designer is coming to visit the crafts center."

"That is great. What is the bad news?" I asked.

"The bad news is that he is coming the day of your class party," said Mommy. "I am so sorry, but I will have to miss it."

"Miss it? How can my own mother miss the Mother's Day party?" I said.

"Karen, this work appointment is very important. Are all the other working mothers taking the day off for the party?" asked Mommy.

"No," I replied.

"I would have been happy to come if it were a regular workday," said Mommy. "But this is my only chance to meet this designer."

This was turning out to be a very hard day. But I understood why Mommy could not come to the party. She works at the Stoneybrook Crafts Center making jewelry.

She needs to be discovered by a famous jewelry designer.

"I understand," I said.

"Thank you, Karen," said Mommy. "Maybe you could ask Elizabeth."

"You are right. I will ask her right now!" I replied.

"I hope she says yes," said Mommy. "I love you and I will talk to you soon."

I was sorry Mommy could not come. But it would be fun to have Elizabeth at the party. I found her in her room, reading a magazine.

"May I come in?" I asked. "I want to invite you to a party!"

"I would love to go to a party with you," said Elizabeth. "Whose party is it? And when?"

"It is our class Mother's Day party. Mommy was going to come, but she cannot leave work," I said. "It is this Friday afternoon."

"I am so sorry, Karen," said Elizabeth.

"But I have an important meeting on Friday. If it were a regular day, I would have been happy to take some time off."

"I know. That is what Mommy said too," I replied.

"I really am sorry," said Elizabeth. "Do you think Nannie might like to come?"

"She is busy," I replied. "But that is okay. I will find someone to come to the party."

The truth was, I was tired of asking people. I was tired of feeling disappointed. But I had promised Hank I would find a grown-up for him to bring to the party. That meant I had to find at least one person.

I hoped Hank would not mind sharing that person with me.

12

Do Not Worry!

The next person I thought of asking to the party was Kristy. She is a very good big sister and she always tries her best to take care of me.

I went to my sister's room. She was not there. Then I remembered that she had a baby-sitting job. I would have to ask her the next day.

At school the next day, I tried to keep my distance from Hank. I did not want to tell him the bad news about Nannie until I had good news from Kristy.

"Class, I would like you to review your work folders," said Ms. Colman. "Please pick a project you are proud of. We will display those projects on our Mother's Day bulletin board."

Good. That was a sit-at-your-desk project. I sit in the front of the room. Hank sits in the back. So I was safe.

At lunchtime I made sure I was surrounded by my friends at all times. I sat between Hannie and Nancy in the cafeteria.

"I am going to get a drink of water," said Hannie.

"No! You cannot leave. There will be an empty seat next to me. Hank might sit down," I said.

"But I am thirsty," said Hannie.

"Here, drink my apple juice," I replied.

I was thirsty too. But I did not care. I was giving my juice away for a worthy cause.

After recess Ms. Colman announced that it was class cleanup time.

"I am going to divide you into two groups," said Ms. Colman. "One group

56

will go outside to clap erasers. The other group will stay here and straighten up our shelves."

Ms. Colman called our names. I got lucky again. Hank's name was called to go outside and clap erasers. I got to stay in and straighten the shelves. (I was so relieved that I did an extra-good job.)

I did not cross paths with Hank all afternoon. I was about to step on the bus to go home when I felt a tap on my shoulder. I turned around.

"Hi, Karen. I have wanted to talk to you all day," said Hank.

Boo. There was no way out. I answered him in my most cheerful voice. "Do not worry," I said. "I kept my promise. I asked Nannie about the party."

That was not enough for Hank.

"Well, what did she say?" he asked.

"She said no," I replied. "But I will invite Kristy tonight. I know she will be happy to be our guest."

"*Our* guest?" said Hank. "But you already

have a guest. You have your mom. I thought the other guest would be for me."

"Um, there has been a little change of plans," I said. "Mommy cannot come. My stepmother cannot come. Nannie cannot come. You and I are in the same boat."

"I sure hope Kristy will say yes. Maybe she can bring a friend. That way we could each have someone at the party," said Hank.

"Do not worry!" I replied. "Something will work out. I, Karen Brewer, am on the case."

13

An Unusual Guest

That afternoon I decided to walk one dog at a time again. It was easier. But it still took awhile. It was too late for me to go to Hannie's for the TV special. Boo. But at least I could still talk to Kristy.

When I walked into the house, Kristy was getting ready to go out.

"I need to talk to you," I said. "It is important."

"Can you talk while I am getting ready? I cannot be late for my baby-sitting job," Kristy replied.

"I am sure you can get ready and answer my question at the same time," I said. "Here is the first part of my question. Do you think you could get out of school on Friday afternoon?"

"I do not have to get out of school," said Kristy. "We already have a half day on Friday."

"All right! Can you come to my class Mother's Day party? I know you are not my mother. But Mommy cannot come. And Elizabeth and Nannie cannot come. You are the next-best mother I have."

"Thank you very much for asking, Karen," said Kristy. "I would love to come if I were free. But I am not. I already made plans. And I am sorry, but I cannot change them."

Bullfrogs! I was starting to feel upset. I felt bad that no one could come to my party. And I had told Hank not to worry because I would find us a guest.

"What am I going to do?" I asked. "I really need to bring someone."

"Sam and Charlie have Friday afternoon off too. You can ask one of them," said Kristy.

"But kids will be bringing their mothers and their aunts and sisters. Women like that. I do not want to bring two *guys*," I said.

"What is the difference? It is only a party. Guys can help celebrate Mother's Day too," Kristy replied.

You know what? She was right. Mrs. Colman had not said no boys allowed. Bringing one of my big brothers could be fun. Maybe I would ask both of them. Then Hank and I would each have a guest.

Kristy had her backpack on and was heading out the door.

"Thank you!" I said. "I will go find Charlie and ask him right now."

Charlie had plans for Friday too. I had one big brother left. I found Sam in the den.

"Hi!" I said. "I know that you have Friday afternoon off from school. Would you like to come to my class party?"

"Karen, I really wanted to use that afternoon to catch up on my schoolwork. Can you find someone else?" asked Sam.

"No. Everyone else I have asked is busy."

"What kind of party is it, anyway?" asked Sam.

"Um, it is a Mother's Day party," I said. "But you do not have to be a mother to come!"

"That is a good thing for me," said Sam.

"Will you come? Please?"

I asked as sweetly as I could. I was asking for Hank and for me.

"I am thinking," said Sam.

Hmm. I needed to do something to make it worthwhile for Sam to come to my party.

"I know what! I will pay you!" I said.

"I could use the money. But I could not take money from my little sister," said Sam.

"Sure you could. You would be doing a job for me. So I will pay you," I said. "And truly I do not mind. I am walking lots of dogs. I have the money. You would really be helping me. And my friend Hank. He does not have anyone to bring to the party either."

"All right," said Sam. "If you are sure you do not mind. I will come to the party and I will let you pay me."

"Thank you!" I said. "Thank you very much. I promise you will have a good time."

I decided to call Hank. I wanted to share the good news with him as soon as I could. There was no answer. I would have to wait and tell him at school in the morning.

I went to my room and wrote a note to myself in my planner. It said: *Buy gifts soon!*

There was not much time left till Mother's Day. I needed to go shopping. But first I had to make a little more money. And I had to do a little more thinking about what to buy.

Money Troubles

On Wednesday when I got to school, I told Hank about Sam. (I did not tell him I had to pay Sam to come as our guest. I did not think Hank would like that.)

"You invited a guy to a Mother's Day party?" said Hank.

"Why not? Ms. Colman did not say we could not do that," I replied. "Sam is fun. You will have a good time. I promise."

"All right," said Hank. "Thanks."

Hank did not look too happy. But he knew it was the best we could do.

"Please open your math workbooks," said Ms. Colman.

I opened my book. But my mind was not on the math in my book. The numbers I was thinking about were dollars and cents.

That morning before school I had tried to figure out my money. When I subtracted the money I needed to buy two great gifts from the money I expected to earn, there was not much left over. There was no way I could buy the kinds of gifts I wanted and still pay Sam to come to the party.

Ms. Colman was giving our class a multiplication problem. As soon as I finished it, I switched back to my own math problem. I kept adding and subtracting. How much did I want to spend on gifts? How much did I need to pay Sam? How much was I going to earn?

What I earned was always less than what I wanted to spend.

We had just finished our math work when Mr. Mackey showed up.

"Good morning, everyone," he said. "Today you are going to start painting the hands you made."

"What are you going to paint on your hand?" asked Natalie.

"I do not know. I am still thinking about it," I replied.

I had not thought about it at all yet. I had been so busy walking dogs and worrying about money and party guests that I had forgotten about the project.

I picked up my papier-mâché hand and stared at it. When I started seeing dollars and cents signs written on the papier-mâché, I knew I was in trouble.

Then I thought of something. Maybe I did not have to earn all the money right away. Maybe I could borrow some money from Daddy and pay him back later. All I had to do was get more dog-walking jobs. That way I could pay Daddy back fast.

But did I have time to walk more dogs? I was already missing important things like after-school specials and I *really* missed seeing my friends.

There was only one way I could sign up more dogs. I would have to do my job better. I would have to be super-speedy. It had not worked the first time. But I had been doing the job for a little while now, so I felt sure I could get the dogs to move faster.

Okay, dogs. Get ready. Starting this afternoon, we are going to walk like we have never walked before!

Where's Maggie?

I picked up Duke first.

"Hello, Duke! How is my good dog?" I asked.

Woof! Duke was happy. So was I. I had a new, improved dog-walking plan. I explained it to Duke while I put on his leash.

"We are going to walk faster today. Walking fast is extra-good exercise," I said. "Come on. I will show you!"

I led Duke out the door and closed it behind me. He was pulling to run to the sidewalk.

"Wait," I said. "I have to double-lock the door."

I reached into my pouch for the key. But I did not feel it. My heart did a flip-flop. Where was it? I had used the key to open the door. Then what had I done with it?

I did not remember putting it back in my pouch. I looked through the window. The key was sitting on the hall table. I had been rushing so much that I had left it there. Now I was locked out.

I remembered that my family keeps an extra set of keys for the Hsus. Thank goodness.

"Come on, Duke," I said. "We have to go to my house."

Duke did not want to go to my house. He wanted to walk around the block the way we always did.

"All right," I said. I followed him down the street. When we finished our walk around the block, I checked my watch. There was no time to go home for the extra keys. I did not want to be late for my next job.

"You will just have to come with me," I said to Duke.

I went to the Kilbournes' and picked up Astrid. Walking Duke and Astrid was just as hard as before. All they wanted to do was roll around and play. By the time they were ready to walk, I was already late for my next appointment.

I could not figure out which would be worse: walking all the dogs at once, or arriving late to pick up a dog.

I decided being late was worse. I did not want any messy accidents.

"Come on, Duke. Come on, Astrid," I said.

We picked up Maggie next. At first she was a little scared of Astrid and Duke. They are much bigger than she is. But they are very friendly dogs. Soon Maggie was jumping up and trying to play with them.

"Not now!" I said. "We have to get Gracie and Garbo."

I picked them up and then counted the number of leashes I was holding. I counted five leashes and five dogs. What was I thinking?

"Attention, everyone!" I said. "It is very important that you all listen to me."

Suddenly there was a tug on one of the leashes. Duke had spotted a squirrel. He started after it. The other dogs followed. I had to wrap my arms around a tree so I would not be pulled down the street. How did I ever think I could walk all these dogs at once?

When the dogs stopped pulling, I unwrapped myself from the tree. Then I unwrapped the leashes that were tangled around my ankles. I was so confused. I did not even know which leash belonged to which dog!

I decided to count the leashes. There were five. Then I counted the dogs. One, two, three, four. No! There had to be a mistake. But how could there be? I am very good at counting. I tried again. I counted only four dogs! That is when I saw an empty collar hanging from one of the leashes.

It was Maggie's collar. She had slipped out of it and was trotting down the street all by herself.

"Maggie, come back!" I called.

But Maggie is a puppy. Puppies slip out of collars. And puppies do not always listen well.

I was scared. What if she ran into the street? A car might hit her. I had to run after her. But I could not leave the other dogs behind. And now they were lying down and would not move. Even if I could make them come with me, Maggie might get scared and run farther away.

I needed help. Fast.

16

Daddy to the Rescue

Somehow I convinced Astrid to stand up. The other dogs followed. I quickly led them to my house. On the way it started to rain. By the time I walked in the door, I was soaking wet. So were the dogs. All four dogs shook themselves off in our hallway.

In no time, Nannie was there with an armful of towels.

Then Daddy came out of his office.

"Karen, what happened?" asked Daddy. "Why are all these dogs here?"

Just then, Shannon came racing down the

75

stairs. She must have been in David Michael's room. David Michael was right behind her.

"I need help!" I said. "You know the Kormans' puppy, Maggie? She got out of her leash and ran away!"

"It was smart of you to come home," said Daddy. "Stay here and help Nannie with these dogs. David Michael and I will go look for Maggie."

"Take treats!" I said.

"Excellent idea," said Daddy.

I was glad to hear that. Everything else I was doing seemed to be wrong.

Daddy and David Michael put on slickers and hurried outside to look for Maggie. Nannie and I gave the other dogs treats and water.

"I hope they find Maggie soon," I said. "I do not know what I would do if something happened to her."

Thank goodness we did not have to wait very long. A few minutes later Daddy and

David Michael returned with Maggie trotting between them.

"Maggie, I am so happy to see you!" I said. I thanked Daddy and David Michael.

"We thought Maggie might have gone home," said Daddy. "So we looked there first. We found her sleeping under a bush in her yard. She came out to get the treat."

"No one was at the Kormans' house, so we brought her back here," said David Michael.

Elizabeth walked in then. She was greeted by Shannon and five other dogs. We told her the whole story.

"I think I know where the Hsus' extra key is," said Elizabeth. "I will go find it for you."

"I guess it is time for me to take the dogs home," I said.

"David Michael and I will keep you company," said Daddy.

Things were looking a lot better. Maggie was safe. I had the key to the Hsus' house. It had even stopped raining.

When we got home again, Daddy asked if he could talk to me in his office.

"Karen, why were you walking so many dogs?" he asked.

I reminded him that I had wanted money to buy presents for Mommy and Elizabeth.

"Remember, you told me I might be able to find more dogs to walk. Well, I did. It was easy," I said.

Then I told Daddy about Hank and how I was going to help him. "His mother lives in Florida. He does not have anyone to bring to the party. So I asked Sam to come. I promised I would pay him. And so now I need even more money."

"You are trying very hard to be nice to everyone," said Daddy. "But I think you have taken on too much at once."

"I think you are right," I replied.

Daddy helped me decide what to do. I would keep walking Duke until the Hsus came home. Then I would walk dogs only when I had the time and someone really needed me.

"Here is one more idea," said Daddy. "How about taking me to the party instead of Sam? You will not have to pay me anything. I would love to come."

"Really?" I said.

"Really," said Daddy. "And I will be happy to help you buy nice gifts for Mommy and Elizabeth. That way you will not have to walk so many dogs."

"I am glad I came home when I needed help," I said.

"You can *always* come to me when you need help, Karen," said Daddy.

I put my arms around Daddy's neck and hugged him.

"Thank you," I replied.

A Secret Phone Call

On Thursday afternoon Mr. Mackey helped us finish making our papier-mâché hands. I had spent our last art class doodling and worrying. So now I had to work fast.

I looked at the hand I had made. An idea was coming to me. I had been walking five dogs. I would draw one dog on each finger.

My drawings did not look exactly like the real dogs. But they were cute and I liked them. And I drew five leashes down to the palm of my papier-mâché hand.

I turned to Natalie and wagged my hand.

"Woof! Woof!" I said.

"That is so cool," said Natalie.

"I like your hand too," I replied.

I looked at Hank's hand. He was drawing a few different things. I saw a baseball, a car, a kite, and a dog. I was not sure why.

"What are you drawing?" I asked.

"I am drawing things I like to do with my dad. We play catch. We go for rides in his car. Last week we flew a kite. And we walk our dog, Jake, together every morning," said Hank.

"It looks good," I said.

Hmm. Hank's hand gave me an idea. I had not told him that I was bringing Daddy to our party. I had just told him we had a new guest who would be a surprise. Now I had an idea about how to make the surprise even better.

That afternoon, after I walked Duke and Astrid, I made a secret phone call. It was to Hank's house. I dialed his number. The phone rang once. It rang twice. Hank answered. Boo. I did not want to talk to Hank. I did not want him to know I was calling. I had to use a phony voice. I tried to sound like a salesperson. I talked loud and fast.

"Good evening! Is this the Reubens' residence?" I said.

"Um, who is calling?" said Hank.

"I need to speak with the head of the household," I replied.

"Just a minute," said Hank.

He put Mr. Reubens on the phone.

"Hello?" said Mr. Reubens.

I switched back to my regular voice.

"Hi, this is Karen Brewer calling, but I do not want Hank to know. It is a surprise," I said.

Mr. Reubens played along.

"Yes, I see," he replied.

"Thank you, Mr. Reubens," I said.

I explained why I was calling. I told him that Daddy was coming to the Mother's Day party. I asked if he could come too.

"I think Hank would be really happy if you were there," I said. "Neither of us thought about asking our fathers to the party."

"Yes, that sounds excellent," said Mr. Reubens. "Just give me the details and you can sign me up."

I told him to be outside school at two o'clock.

"I will tell Daddy to meet you there," I said. "That way you can come in together."

"Thank you for calling," said Mr. Reubens.

I had done it. I had invited guests for me and for Hank. Now all I needed to do was think of presents for Mommy and Elizabeth. This was going to be the best Mother's Day ever!

Party!

On Friday, Ms. Colman helped us put our papier-mâché hands on the display board. At the end of the day, we would be allowed to take them home. I was glad. There was someone I wanted to give my hand to on Sunday.

We were all so excited that we could hardly get through the day. We started setting up for the party right after lunch. The first guests began to arrive at quarter to two.

"Who is our guest going to be?" asked Hank. "Can you tell me now?"

"No way! You will see soon enough," I replied.

I was busy talking to some of the other guests when I saw Daddy's face at the door. Mr. Reubens was beside him. Hank was talking to Ricky and did not see them.

"Excuse me, but you have a visitor," I said to Hank.

Hank looked up. A huge smile spread across his face. He ran to his dad and hugged him. I was right behind him.

"Hi, Daddy! Hi, Mr. Reubens," I said. "What do you think of the surprise, Hank?"

"I think it is great," Hank replied. "Thanks, Karen."

I did not see much of Hank after that. He was busy making sure his dad got to talk to everyone at the party. I could see he was proud of his dad. That made me happy. This had turned out to be a good surprise.

Hank was not the only one who got a surprise at our Mother's Day party. My whole class got a surprise from Ms. Colman.

First Mr. Simmons walked in. (He is Ms.

Colman's husband.) He was carrying their baby, Jane. Beside him was an older woman. She looked very familiar.

"Class, I know you have met Mr. Simmons and Jane before," said Ms. Colman. "Now I would like you to meet my mother, Dorothy Colman. She has come from Chicago to visit us."

That was it! The woman was Ms. Colman's mother. I had met her at Ms. Colman's wedding. (I had been one of Ms. Colman's flower girls.)

Ms. Colman invited her *own* mother to our party.

"Hi," I said. "Do you remember me? I was a flower girl in Ms. Colman's wedding."

"Of course I remember you, Karen," said Ms. Colman's mom. "You are not easy to forget. In fact, you remind me quite a bit of my daughter when she was your age."

"I do?" I said. "How?"

This was very exciting. I could not believe that Ms. Colman was like me. I wanted to

hear all about Ms. Colman when she was my age.

"She had lots of energy, just like you," said Ms. Colman's mom. "And when she spoke too loudly in the house, I had to remind her to use her indoor voice."

So that is where Ms. Colman got the idea! She had needed reminding too.

Ms. Colman stepped up to us then. "Hi, Mom. Are you telling stories about me?" she said.

"Of course I am!"

Ms. Colman and her mother told the class lots of funny stories. She was not the only one who had stories to tell. Mothers and fathers and cousins and friends were at the party. Everyone had stories. And everyone had a great time.

The Perfect Presents

I had not had much time to think about the presents I wanted to get for Mommy and Elizabeth. And now it was Saturday. Nannie was taking David Michael, Andrew, and me downtown to shop. We piled into the Pink Clinker. (That is the name of Nannie's old car.)

"Does anyone know what they are buying?" asked Nannie. "If not, we can just browse."

We voted to browse. We started off at Bellair's department store. The bracelet and scarf I liked were both gone. I did not see anything else I wanted to buy. Neither did David Michael or Andrew.

We passed a bookstore. Mommy and Elizabeth like books a lot. But I did not know what they had already read.

We passed a flower shop. Lots of cute things besides flowers were for sale. But none of us saw anything we wanted to buy.

Then we passed a stationery store.

"I need to buy a card," said David Michael.

So we went inside.

"I found what I want!" said Andrew. "Look!"

We all looked where he was pointing — at a shelf of cross-eyed bears. They came in different colors. They looked pretty silly to me. But I did not say a word.

"Those are lovely," said Nannie. "Which colors would you like to get?"

"The red one and the green one," said Andrew.

"You picked very nice ones," said Nannie.

I still did not know what to get. But I found some very pretty wrapping paper. It was pink with purple flowers. Then I found a funny card for Mommy. On the outside it said, *What is the best thing about Mother's Day?* When I opened it, two hands popped out holding the word *You!*

I got a different card for Elizabeth. The outside said, *Thank you for being so special.* The inside said, *Happy Mother's Day.* I decided I would draw hearts and flowers around the words.

But I could not just give Mommy and Elizabeth cards and wrapping paper. I had worked so hard to make money to buy presents. What was I going to buy? Then I saw them. The perfect presents.

They were near the checkout counter. They were the prettiest planners I had ever seen. They were much prettier than the one I had bought for myself. One was decorated with white roses. The other looked like a patchwork quilt. Mommy and Elizabeth each had such busy schedules. I was sure these were presents they could use.

I took out all the money I had earned. Then I added a little bit of the money that Daddy had lent me. I handed it to the cashier.

"These are lovely," she said when she was putting the planners into a bag. "You have very good taste."

"I know," I replied. "Thank you!"

Happy Mother's Day

I wanted to leave the gifts out as long as possible so I could look at them. So I did not wrap them until Sunday morning.

Then I went downstairs to help get ready for our brunch. When I walked into the dining room, Daddy was there putting flowers on the table.

"Good morning!" he said.

"Where is everyone?" I asked.

"Nannie and Elizabeth went out for a walk. Sam, Charlie, and Kristy went to the store for food. And David Michael and Andrew are still upstairs," said Daddy.

"I will be right back!" I said.

I ran upstairs. I had wrapped one other gift. It was for Daddy. This seemed like a good time to give it to him. I went downstairs again and put it on the desk in his office. Then I ran back to the dining room.

"Daddy, could you please come into your office for a minute?" I said.

Daddy looked puzzled, but followed me to his office.

"Happy Mother's Day!" I said.

"Why, Karen, you do not have to give me a gift," said Daddy.

"I did not have to. But I wanted to. This would not have been such a happy Mother's Day for me without your help," I said. "I wanted to thank you."

Daddy opened his gift.

"It is the hand you made at school. Thank you so much. I love it!" said Daddy.

He put it right on top of his bookcase.

"I will look at it and enjoy it all the time," said Daddy. "And now I would like to give a present to you."

I looked around the office. I did not see anything wrapped up in gift paper.

"My gift to you is a raise in your allowance," said Daddy. "You have been working very hard to make money to do nice things for other people. It is good to work to earn money. But you need to leave time for other things. You need time for homework. And you need time to have fun with your friends."

I felt gigundoly proud and grown-up. I felt that I had earned the raise in my allowance.

"Thank you, Daddy," I said.

"I would like you to promise me something," said Daddy. "I would like you to promise that you will always come to me when you need help, no matter what it is."

"I promise," I replied.

"Then it is a deal. I have a promise and you have a raise," said Daddy.

We shook hands to seal our deal. Then we heard a car door slam.

"That must be your brothers and sister with the food. Come on, we have a lot to do before Nannie and Elizabeth get back," said Daddy.

David Michael and Andrew must have heard the car door too. They were both heading downstairs to help. Soon Nannie and Elizabeth would return. They would find a beautiful room filled with balloons and flowers and good food. They would have lots of presents to open. And they would get lots of hugs.

Later, Andrew and I would visit Mommy and Seth.

It was going to be a happy Mother's Day for sure.

L. GODWIN

About the Author

ANN M. MARTIN lives in New York City and loves animals, especially cats. She has two cats of her own, Gussie and Woody.

Other books by Ann M. Martin that you might enjoy are *Stage Fright; Me and Katie (the Pest)*; and the books in *The Baby-sitters Club* series.

Ann likes ice cream and *I Love Lucy*. And she has her own little sister, whose name is Jane.

Little Sister

Don't miss # 122
KAREN'S COWBOY

"That was Granny Engle on the phone," explained Seth.

"How is she?" I asked.

"She is terrific," said Seth. "Especially since she has just won a trip to Colorado!"

My mouth fell open.

"Granny entered a raffle at a fair," Seth went on. "She won the grand prize, which is a trip for four people to go to a dude ranch for a week. As a special gift, she wants to send the four of us!"

"Oh my goodness!" I said.

"It sounds like fun," said Mommy.

"But what is a dude ranch?" asked Andrew.

"A dude ranch is a place where you can go and ride horses and live like a real old-time cowboy," explained Mommy.

"Oh boy!" I shouted. Then I thought of something. "But there are no school vacations coming up," I said. "How can I go?"

"I will have to call Ms. Colman," said Mommy. "We will ask for special permission for you to miss school. But you will have to make up the work you miss," she warned me.

"Oh boy!" I shouted again. I started to jump up and down. I did not mind the idea of making up all the work. I was too excited about being a real cowgirl!

BABY-SITTERS™
Little Sister

by Ann M. Martin
author of The Baby-sitters Club®

More Titles... ➡

Available wherever you buy books, or use this order form.

Scholastic Inc., P.O. Box 7502, Jefferson City, MO 65102

Please send me the books I have checked above. I am enclosing $_____ (please add $2.00 to cover shipping and handling). Send check or money order – no cash or C.O.Ds please.

Name_____Birthdate_____

Address_____

City_____State/Zip_____

Please allow four to six weeks for delivery. Offer good in U.S.A. only. Sorry, mail orders are not available to residents of Canada. Prices subject to change.

BSLS998